THE DISAPPEARING CARD TRICK

Elizabeth Bryan Mysteries

Vicki Berger Erwin

SAINT LOUIS

To Libby and Bryan, with love
Mom

Elizabeth Bryan Mysteries
The Disappearing Card Trick
The Case of the Questionable Cousin

Cover illustration by Sally Schaedler

Copyright © 1996 Concordia Publishing House
3558 S. Jefferson Avenue, St. Louis, MO 63118-3968
Manufactured in the United States of America

Library of Congress Cataloging-in-Publication Data

Ervin, Vicki Berger, 1951–
    The disappearing card trick/Vicki Berger Erwin
        p.   cm.—(Elizabeth Bryan mysteries)
    Summary: When the most valuable baseball card of Elizabeth's collection disappears, her mother's first new date and a suspicious baseball card dealer are likely suspects.
    ISBN 0-570-04835-4
    [1. Baseball cards—Fiction. 2. Baseball—Fiction. 3. Christian life—Fiction. 4. Mystery and detective stories.] I. Title. II. Series.
PZ7.E7445Di 1996
[Fic]—dc20   95-22850

2 3 4 5 6 7 8 9 10   05 04 03 02 01 00 99 98 97 96

CONTENTS

1
BASEBALL CARDS
ARE WORTH
MONEY?

Elizabeth spread Dad's baseball cards in long, even rows across the front porch. Her younger brother, Mike, followed along behind her on his hands and knees, oohing and aahing over each one. It was the first time Mike had ever seen the collection and the first time for Elizabeth to explain each player the way Dad would have. She knew Dad would want her to share everything he'd ever told her about the cards with Mike.

"I know that one!" Mike said, picking up a picture of a player wearing a St. Louis Cardinals uniform. "It's Stan the Man Musial. He's the statue in front of Busch Stadium. These are cool."

Elizabeth got to the last card. She held it for a moment before placing it in the row. Pete White—Dad's favorite player, even though he'd played only a few seasons. He could pitch and hit, something Dad said happened about as often as the Chicago Cubs playing in the World Series. The thing about him that fascinated her dad, and her, was that after three winning seasons, Pete White retired from the game. Dad and she had always wondered where he'd gone after that. And who quits the game in their prime anyway? Dad always asked.

Mike jumped up, breaking into Elizabeth's memories and scattering the baseball cards. "Mr. Hamilton! Look, Elizabeth, it's my baseball coach."

He pulled the screen door open, making the hinges creak like they might part from the frame. "Mom! Mom!" he shouted, "my baseball coach is here." Mike disappeared inside the house, letting the door slam behind him and leaving Elizabeth alone to greet the visitor.

A tall, dark-haired man got out of a black Volvo station wagon and started up Elizabeth's front walk. He was carrying a white plastic bag. He paused at the bottom of the porch steps. "Does Mike Bryan live here?" he asked. When he smiled at her, his white teeth shone against his tanned skin and his blue eyes sparkled. "He must. The two of you have to be brother and sister! That red hair and those freckles."

Elizabeth stood up, knowing that her face must be almost as red as her hair. Why did everyone have to notice her freckles first thing? She looked over her shoulder. "He's in the house. Let me get him."

At that moment, Mike flew out the door and down the steps. The man had to back-step quickly to keep from being bowled over by the small boy. "Hey, there," he said, reaching out and punching Mike lightly on the shoulder.

"My uniform! I'll bet you finally got me a uniform," Mike said, pulling on the bag.

"Honestly, Mikey," Elizabeth scolded. "Remember your manners."

"And you remember to call me Mike," her brother answered.

The screen creaked again, and Mom stepped out on the porch. Elizabeth noticed Mom had brushed her blonde hair and put on a fresh coat of lipstick. She took another look at the man Mike was crawling all over.

"Mike, get off Mr. Hamilton right this minute," Mom said.

"It's okay, Lydia. He's had to wait a long time for this, and I'm glad to see he's excited about it." The baseball coach had squatted down beside Mike and was unpacking the midget-sized uniform. They'd had to order an extra-small size for him.

Mr. Hamilton held the shirt up against Mike's chest. Mike stepped back and stripped off his T-shirt, then reached for the uniform shirt.

"Mom, can't you do something about him?" Elizabeth asked, covering her eyes. Her little brother was standing half-naked in the front yard where anyone could see him.

"Hey, Mr. Hamilton! What are you doing here?" a boy's voice called out. A bicycle swerved off the sidewalk and into the yard, braking to a stop just inches from the porch.

Now Elizabeth knew she was going to die. It was Justin Thayer, their paperboy and possibly the cutest boy in her whole class. She quickly smoothed her hair. She wished she'd had Mom trim her bangs last night. They were hanging in her eyes and must be making her look like a shaggy dog.

"Mike, bud, you live here?" Justin asked.

By then, Mike had managed to twist himself up in his uniform. "Help, help," he mumbled from underneath the shirt.

Justin let his bike fall to the ground and quickly untangled Mike. "Astros," he said. "Best team in the league—always has been, at least since I was on it in first grade. It always will be—as long as Mr. Hamilton and I are the coaches."

Mike thrust his chest forward proudly displaying the logo.

Elizabeth couldn't believe what she was hearing. Why hadn't she ever gone to one of Mike's games or practices? She would have if anyone had bothered to mention Justin.

"Don, would you like a glass of iced tea? It's so nice of you to make a special trip over here to bring Mike's uniform. We could have picked it up at practice," Mom said.

She'd had a smile on her face ever since she'd stepped outside. When Mr. Hamilton, Don as Mom called him, looked up at her, her cheeks turned pink. Elizabeth realized she'd missed out on more than seeing Justin at Mike's baseball practices and games. This wasn't like her mom at all. And Elizabeth didn't like it much.

"Tea would be great," Mr. Hamilton answered, starting up the steps.

"Wait!" Elizabeth held up her hands to block his way. She stooped and gathered the baseball cards into a pile. Even she knew it wasn't good for the cards to be stepped on.

"Justin, come see Stan the Man. My dad has

his card," Mike said, pulling on the older boy's hand.

"Stan Musial?" said Justin, a touch of awe in his voice. "Really?" He followed Mike up onto the porch.

"Hi, Elizabeth," he said.

"Hi, Justin," she managed to answer without stuttering. She rubbed the baseball cards she was holding back and forth against one another.

"I didn't know you and Mike lived around here," Justin said as he sat down on the porch. "We just moved onto the next block."

We've been on your paper route for the past year, Elizabeth thought, but didn't say. "Welcome to the neighborhood," she said instead. "How do you like it?"

"It's okay, but I miss Heath and Eric and some of the others who live on my old street. There aren't any guys my age around here."

Justin turned his attention to the baseball cards, picking up one and looking at it, then setting it aside and picking up another. He let out a low whistle and held up a single card.

"Pete White," he said. "Where'd you get this one?"

"It was my dad's," Elizabeth said, daring to move a little closer. "It was his favorite."

"I'll bet," said Justin. "This is in great shape. It's worth $500, maybe $1000, easy!"

Elizabeth leaned forward and peered at the card. Money? These cards were worth money? And if Justin knew what he was talking about, a lot of money.

"What'd you say about Pete White?" Mr. Hamilton stood over them.

"Look at this." Justin handed him the card.

Elizabeth had to stop herself from reaching out and grabbing it away from Mr. Hamilton.

"He was one of my favorite players," Mr. Hamilton said. "I used to have this same card when I was a kid. It was such a mystery when he disappeared. I wonder what happened to him? I wonder what happened to my card?"

He shook his head and handed Elizabeth's card back to Justin. "I would have been a little more careful about where I stuck it if I'd known that it was going to be worth money someday."

"You like baseball cards?" Justin asked Elizabeth.

Her throat went dry and she swallowed hard. "Sure," Elizabeth said with a shrug. She *did* like her dad's baseball cards. "The Pete White is one of my favorites too. I wonder whatever became of him? I mean to play so great for a couple of years, then give it all up."

"I think he must have had an accident," Mr. Hamilton said. "It could have made it impossible for him to play, but he didn't want any pity."

Elizabeth continued to look at Justin, waiting for him to answer.

"I don't have a clue," Justin finally said. "But it sure did make his card worth a lot because there weren't that many of them."

"Elizabeth," Mom said, "are those your dad's cards?"

Like Dad was going to come back any minute and claim them, Elizabeth thought. He'd been dead for five years. Elizabeth had come across the cards in the back of a closet and had taken them out whenever she missed her dad. This morning she'd decided to show them to Mike.

"Mike, you a baseball card fan too?" Mr. Hamilton asked, resting his hand on Mike's tangled hair.

"I have my own collection," Mike said.

Mr. Hamilton looked at Mom, then at Elizabeth, then at Mike. "I have an idea. There's a big card show this weekend. I'm busy on Saturday, but how about I take you to see it on Sunday? You too, Justin. I think Ozzie Smith is going to be there signing autographs."

"The Wizard?" Mike gasped. His mouth hung open and he stared blankly into the distance. "I could shake his hand?"

"Maybe even get your picture taken with him," said Mr. Hamilton. "I'll pick everybody up at 10 a.m. How about it? We could have lunch, make a day of it."

"In the morning?" Elizabeth asked. "Sunday morning?" She glanced at Mom who was still smiling.

"Bright and early," Mr. Hamilton said.

"Can't," Elizabeth said. "We have church."

"That's right," Mom said, her smile dimming slightly.

Elizabeth detected her mother's disappointment and was glad they couldn't go. Who did Mr. Hamilton think he was anyway, inviting the whole family to go someplace with him?

"Mom, please. We could miss this one time," Mike pleaded.

"I have to teach Sunday school. You know that," she said softly.

"We can go later," Mr. Hamilton said. "I'll pick you up around one o'clock instead."

He lifted his foot and scratched the back of his leg. Tiger, one of their cats, attacked his loose shoestring. "What the ... ?" Mr. Hamilton shook his foot, and Tiger hung in the air for a moment, then dropped to the ground with a loud yowl.

"Tiger! Kitty!" Elizabeth hurried to calm the cat, but he quickly scurried into the shrubbery growing along the porch. "You hurt him," she accused Mr. Hamilton.

"Sorry. I didn't know what it was and it startled me. It's okay, isn't it? I mean, you can't hurt a cat. They're nothing but overgrown rodents, aren't they?" He smiled as he spoke.

"They are not!" Not only was he a buttin-ski, but he was one who didn't like cats! Elizabeth hoped Mom would say they couldn't go to the baseball card show now that he'd shown his true colors as a cat-hater.

Mom patted Elizabeth's shoulder. "The cat is just fine." She turned to Mr. Hamilton. "One o'clock would be great," she said.

"Justin, can you go?" Mr. Hamilton asked.

Elizabeth held her breath. It wouldn't be totally awful if Justin went.

"Great. Thanks for asking me," Justin said. "I'll meet you here."

"See you at practice tomorrow," Mr. Hamilton said to Mike. "Bye, Lydia, Elizabeth." He waved over his shoulder as he jogged to his car.

Elizabeth waited, hoping he would trip.

"Could you bring some of these cards?" Justin asked. "I know that there will be people at the card show who could give you a good idea of what they're worth. If it's what I think, you'd better start keeping them in plastic cases."

"I was thinking about doing that anyway," Elizabeth said.

Justin stacked the cards and put them back into the box. "Guess I'll see you on Sunday."

Elizabeth nodded. "See you."

Justin picked up his bike, ran across the lawn, then threw his leg over the bar and pedaled away. Elizabeth sighed.

"These cards stay right here at home," Mom said. She tucked the box under her arm.

"I'll be careful," Elizabeth said. "Promise." Justin was counting on her to bring the cards.

"No way. Your dad had these for years and years, and I'm not about to let them get lost or spoiled now."

Elizabeth watched through the screen as Mom put the box on the top shelf of the coat closet. She was sure her mother wouldn't notice if she stuck one or two of the best cards inside her purse and took them to the show—as soon as she got some of those plastic cases Justin had mentioned. What could possibly happen?

2

AN ALMOST
PICTURE-
PERFECT
AFTERNOON

Elizabeth looked at her watch—almost one o'clock. If Justin was going to the baseball card show with them, he'd be here any minute. *If* he really decided to go.

Just in case, she put on one more layer of lip gloss. She'd rather have real lipstick, but Mom was sure to notice. When she dropped the silver tube back into her purse, Elizabeth checked to make sure the Pete White baseball card was still inside the plastic case she'd bought the day before with hard-earned baby-sitting money.

Mom joined Elizabeth at the hall mirror, arranging, then rearranging the navy-and-red scarf she wore. Elizabeth couldn't remember her mother ever wearing a scarf before. Usually she wore a T-shirt and jeans or a casual dress or skirt outfit for work. Today she had on eyeliner, mascara, and—Elizabeth leaned a little closer and sniffed.

"You have on my cologne!" she said.

Mom blushed. "None of mine smelled quite right. Maybe they're all too old or something. You don't mind, do you?"

"But why?" Elizabeth asked. Mom was acting like she was going on a date. Elizabeth drew a sharp breath. Her mother *liked* Mr. Hamilton. Too gross. She peered through the screen door.

Mike sat on the bottom porch step, beating the ground with a stick.

The smile Elizabeth had started to dread appeared on her mother's face as the black Volvo pulled up to the curb. The car door opened and Mr. Hamilton stepped out.

He greeted Mike with a high five. "Sorry I'm late," he said to Mom. "I had a call from one of the baseball team parents just as I was walking out the door." The two of them exchanged looks. "I'll tell you about it later," he added in a low tone directed toward Mom.

"You're not really late. And Justin isn't here yet anyway," Mom said.

Elizabeth felt her face flush. If he wasn't coming, he could have called.

"How long do we have to wait?" Mike asked, whining.

"Not long. I think he's coming now," said Mr. Hamilton. He held the screen door open and Mom walked out. She used her fingers to comb through Mike's reddish hair—an exact middle tone between Mom's light and Elizabeth's darker shades.

"You coming?" Mr. Hamilton continued to hold the door open. He'd cut himself shaving, Elizabeth noticed as she brushed past him and he, too, had on cologne. The car was going to smell like the cosmetics section of a department store.

"Hi," Justin called as he leaned his bike against the porch.

Elizabeth's throat felt so tight all she could manage was a smile.

Mike was already in the backseat of the car. Justin climbed in beside him.

"Mom," Elizabeth said, her throat finally relaxing.

Her mother stopped and turned sharply.

If Mom sat in the front seat with Mr. Hamilton, they'd look like a *family* going out together. Elizabeth didn't want people thinking Mr. Hamilton was connected to her or her mother in any way.

"Could you sit in the back with me?" Elizabeth whispered as she held her mother back.

"What?" Mom's forehead wrinkled for an instant, then smoothed as she glanced at Justin, then at Elizabeth. She grabbed her daughter's hand and squeezed. "Justin, why don't you sit in front with Mr. Hamilton?" Mom called to him.

Justin shrugged, then moved from the back-seat to the front. Mom and Elizabeth climbed into the backseat, one on either side of Mike.

All the way downtown Elizabeth wondered what her dad would think about Mom going out with a man. Elizabeth had to admit he was nice looking, tall, slender, with dark curly hair and blue eyes. But it didn't feel right for her *mother* to be acting like she had a boyfriend.

When they arrived at the convention center, Mr. Hamilton let everyone out at the front door, then went to park the car.

"We'll probably have to wait in a long line for Mike to get Ozzie Smith's autograph," said Mom.

"I'm going to see the Wizard, the wonderful Wizard of Oz," Mike sang as he skipped along beside Mom.

"Is it all right if we go look at some of the booths?" Justin asked.

Elizabeth held her breath, waiting for her mom's answer. Her mother, as overprotective as she was, would probably make her stay in the line right beside her little brother. She wished she'd thought ahead and discussed this with Mom before they got to the show. She didn't want to be embarrassed.

"Of course. I don't want the two of you to have to spend the afternoon standing in line," said Mom. "Go on and have fun. We'll catch up with you later." She gave Elizabeth a gentle shove and winked when Elizabeth pushed her hand away.

Inside the large room, table after table spread before them. Some were covered with piles of baseball cards, some with boxes, and some had display cases. Ozzie Smith sat at a table on a small stage at one end of the room. A line of people waiting to see him wound nearly three-quarters of the way around the hall.

"They won't be getting up to Ozzie very soon," said Justin. "Where should we start?"

"You tell me," said Elizabeth. "This is my first card show."

"Then I'm pleased to introduce you." Justin bowed and spread out his arm as if the room were his to give.

Elizabeth had to laugh. He was wearing a plaid shirt open over a T-shirt, long khaki shorts, and high-topped athletic shoes. He had his baseball hat on backward and a patch of his blond hair stuck straight out through the opening. But his actions were so elegant.

"I usually walk all around once and check prices before I buy anything. Once I bought a card at what I thought was a great price at the first table I stopped at. A couple of tables down it was about a dollar cheaper, and a little farther on it cost half of what I'd paid. You got to make sure you're getting the best deal."

"Competition," said Elizabeth.

Justin nodded his head.

"Hey, over there." Justin pointed at a corner booth formed by two tables covered in red felt cloth and set at angles. In the V the tables made, there was a camera and a screen backdrop. "That's Mr. Becker. He owns the baseball card shop near where we live. And I'm one of his best customers. Did you bring your Pete White card?" Justin grabbed Elizabeth's wrist and pulled her through the crowd.

Elizabeth almost had to run to keep up with him. She'd never realized how tall he was—or maybe he'd grown over the summer. She barely came up to his shoulder.

"Justin! Shouldn't be surprised to see you here!" A tall, very skinny man reached out his bony hand and clamped it on Justin's shoulder. Elizabeth had the feeling his hands would be clammy cold, so when he turned to her, she stepped back out of his reach.

"This little bud is a lot better looking than those thugs you usually bum with," he said, smiling and showing teeth that looked like small kernels of corn.

"This is Elizabeth, and you won't believe the card she's got," Justin said.

Mr. Becker folded his arms across his chest and waited.

"Pete White. She's got a Pete White." Justin nudged her. "Show him. Go ahead."

When Justin said Pete White, Elizabeth noticed a momentary tightening in Mr. Becker. She unzipped her purse and felt around inside for the hard, cold plastic. She pulled out the card and held it up for Mr. Becker to see. Again, she noticed a flicker of interest.

"Ah, but is it real?" the man asked.

Elizabeth felt hot all over. Mr. Becker wasn't playing fair. She knew by the way his eyes had darkened when he looked at the card that he was interested in it, but now he was pretending not to care. She didn't like him much.

"It's real and in great condition," Justin said as he took the card out of Elizabeth's hand and gave it to Mr. Becker.

The baseball card dealer examined the front of the card, bringing it so close to his face it almost touched his nose, then he turned it over and studied the back just as closely.

"Have you ever seen one of these cards before?" Justin asked eagerly. "I couldn't wait for you to see it."

"I've seen one once before," Mr. Becker said, carefully removing the card from its holder.

Elizabeth heard Justin's small sigh and saw disappointment flash across his face. He'd thought he was bringing the dealer something special.

"How much you asking?" Mr. Becker said as he slid the card back into the plastic sleeve.

"What?"

"How much money do you want for the card?" he asked, letting his impatience show.

Elizabeth snatched the card back. "It's not for sale. It belonged to my dad."

"We thought you might have an idea what it was worth," said Justin.

Mr. Becker didn't take his eyes off the card as Elizabeth returned it to her purse. "What's that you say?"

"Value. What's it worth?" Justin said.

"Maybe 500, 600 dollars." Mr. Becker's eyes wandered to a young man who had stepped up to the other table and was looking at some cards displayed in a case.

"That's all?" said Justin.

"That's a lot for a baseball card," said Elizabeth.

"Lady's right," said Mr. Becker, moving a step toward the other customer.

"My price guide said Pete White could be worth as much as $1,500," said Justin.

"Only if someone is willing to pay that much, son," said the card dealer. He glanced at Elizabeth's purse. "I might go as high as $750," he said to her.

She shook her head and tightened her grip on the purse.

"Can I help you?" Mr. Becker leaned toward the young man.

"Just looking," the teenager mumbled.

Justin picked up a card from the table and studied it. He laid it down and picked up another.

"Couldn't interest you kids in having your

picture taken, could I?" Mr. Becker asked. "Make you look like a pro, Justin." He spread out what looked to Elizabeth like an assortment of baseball cards. When she looked a little closer she saw that they were pictures of kids posed to look remarkably like baseball cards.

"These are great," said Justin.

"Special deal for special customers today only. You and the little lady for one low price—three pictures each for $10," said Mr. Becker.

"When did you start doing this?" Justin asked.

"Awhile back. Trying to make a living," said Mr. Becker.

"Elizabeth, you want to?" asked Justin.

"Me? Oh, no." Elizabeth shook her head.

"C'mon, it'll be cool," said Justin.

Before Elizabeth knew what was happening, Mr. Becker was helping her squeeze through an opening between the tables and leading her behind a set of curtains.

There was barely room to turn around inside the curtained cubicle. A rolling rack holding several baseball shirts and a chair took up more than half the space.

"Choose a shirt, put it on, and come out," Mr. Becker said, dropping the curtain.

Elizabeth chose the shirt most familiar to her—St. Louis Cardinals, the hometown team. She slipped it over her navy blue T-shirt, then put the matching hat on her head, taking care to cover her ears and not to mess up her hair too much. She wished there was a mirror.

Elizabeth peeked through the curtain. "I'm ready, I think."

"Come on out." Justin pulled the curtain open. "You look great!"

"The purse has to go. Know any baseball players who carry a purse?" Mr. Becker tossed it back into the dressing area.

"You want to hold a bat or wear a glove?" Justin asked.

Elizabeth picked up the glove. "This one?" she asked, nervously twirling it around.

"Great," Mr. Becker said. "Move against the screen."

"Not that one," said Justin. He pulled down one screen, then another, finally deciding on a ballpark background.

Mr. Becker fiddled with the camera. Justin moved her against the background and told her how to stand.

Mr. Becker clicked a picture.

"Now stand like this." Justin showed her a

second pose, and Elizabeth copied it, smiling at the thought of how silly she must look.

"One more." Justin stretched liked he was reaching for a ball, and Elizabeth copied him.

The camera flashed a third time.

Elizabeth pulled the hat off and shook her head, hoping she hadn't worn the hat long enough to develop "hat hair." She noticed a small crowd had gathered to watch the photo session. Out of the corner of her eye she caught a glimpse of her mother and Mr. Hamilton, laughing and talking in a far corner.

"That was fun," Elizabeth said. She unbuttoned the shirt and pulled it off, quickly hanging it back on the rack in the dressing room.

"Your turn," Elizabeth said to Justin. "Do you mind if I go check in with Mom while you're having your pictures taken?" She hated missing Justin's photo session, but her mom and Mr. Hamilton looked—she wasn't sure what, but they were standing too close together.

"I'll catch up with you when I'm finished here," said Justin, sounding a little disappointed.

Elizabeth smiled at him, and he smiled back.

She pushed her way through the crowd, finally reaching Mom. "Has Mike gotten his autograph yet?" she asked, stepping between her mother and Mr. Hamilton.

"Not yet," said Mom.

"You've been just standing here the whole time?" Elizabeth asked. "How boring!"

"Not really," said Mom.

Elizabeth noticed her mother's eyes were bright and her cheeks were flushed. She was having fun!

"Come on with me and look around a little," said Elizabeth, taking her mom's arm and pulling her away from Mr. Hamilton. "He'll stay with Mike," Elizabeth added.

"Elizabeth!" Mom protested.

"Go ahead," said Mr. Hamilton. "And Elizabeth, if you happen to see any of those Pete White cards, pick up one for me. That really is some special card."

Elizabeth didn't bother to say anything to Mr. Hamilton. She pulled on her Mom's hand again, and this time, Mom followed.

"Elizabeth, Mr. Hamilton is trying to be friendly. Why are you so rude to him?"

Elizabeth rolled her eyes.

"I think we're going to have a little talk," Mom said, "although this is neither the time nor the place. Where's Justin?" she asked, changing the subject.

Elizabeth knew that this wasn't the last she'd hear about Mr. Hamilton, not yet. "Getting his picture taken," she said. She continued to chatter on, pointing out cards, repeating things Justin had told her. Mom stayed close to her, glancing occasionally toward the autograph line.

Elizabeth picked up a flyer with the word *warning* printed in red around the edges. "Look at this." She held it in front of Mom's face. "Baseball cards, sports cards are a much bigger deal than I ever knew. I mean, this is a warning about counterfeit cards. Someone actually has gone to all that trouble to make a little money. If they'd work that hard at a job …"

"Elizabeth!" Mom laughed.

"Isn't that awful?" Justin joined them and pointed at the counterfeit warning. "And I should know because it happened to me this past year. I had a card I traded for, a Ken Griffey Jr., and when I tried to trade it at a shop for something else I wanted, the owner said it was a fake. Boy, did I feel dumb!"

Elizabeth felt a chill. It was one thing to read a warning about counterfeit cards, but it was too real to hear Justin say it had happened to him.

"Mom! Elizabeth! Justin! Look!" Mike waved a piece of paper. "I have Ozzie's picture, and he signed it! I'm going to hang it in my room."

"That's great, Mike," said Elizabeth. She had her eye on Mr. Hamilton who was holding up his camera for Mom to see and nodding.

"Let's go home. I want to show Aunt Nan," said Mike. Aunt Nan lived in the other side of their duplex and, although she wasn't related, was the best aunt in the world.

"Maybe Mr. Hamilton wants to look around," said Mom.

"I've seen all I want to see," Mr. Hamilton said, his eyes on Mom.

Elizabeth's stomach gave a lurch.

On the way home, Mom got in front before Elizabeth had a chance to say anything. Mike talked about Ozzie Smith the entire trip.

When they got to the house, Aunt Nan was on the front porch sitting on the swing. Mike climbed over Elizabeth to get out of the car and ran to Aunt Nan, yelling about his autograph. Mom was slow to climb out. Elizabeth waited.

"Listen, I'll bring those pictures by as soon as I pick them up," Justin said.

For a moment, Elizabeth couldn't figure out what he meant. Then she remembered. "I'm not so sure I want to see mine."

"You were a good sport about it. And don't worry—you were a natural." Justin climbed on his bike and rode off, the compliments leaving Elizabeth feeling warm all over.

"Did you have fun?" Mom put her arm around Elizabeth as they climbed the porch steps together.

"Um-hmm," Elizabeth said.

"I take it from the expressions on your faces that the two of you had a good time too," said Aunt Nan.

"Fun," said Mom.

Elizabeth nodded.

"Lydia, you look like a kid. Having a boyfriend has done wonders for you," Aunt Nan said.

Elizabeth pulled away. Her mother's face was bright red. "Mom doesn't have a boyfriend."

"A manfriend, then," said Aunt Nan, her blue eyes dancing. "Think he can fix me up?" She patted her white curls.

"Nan!" Mom giggled.

Elizabeth's mouth dropped open. Her mother sounded like her and her best friend, Meghan, when they talked about boys.

"Did he say anything about another date?" Aunt Nan asked.

"Dinner. Thursday," Mom said. "Can you watch the kids?"

"Of course!" Aunt Nan agreed with a clap of her hands.

"Mom, Thursday. You can't!" Elizabeth couldn't believe it. Her mom had a date. And on their night.

"Sweetie, I forgot." Mom's hand covered her mouth. "Our dance class."

On Thursday night, Elizabeth and her mother took a tap-dance class together. It was one of Elizabeth's favorite times of the week. She'd thought it was one of Mom's too.

"You can teach her whatever you learn that night, Elizabeth," Aunt Nan said.

"I can't go without Mom."

"I'll try to make it," Mom said quickly. "Maybe we can have an early dinner."

"You can miss one class," said Aunt Nan. "You go with Don and have fun."

"Mom, you promised," said Elizabeth.

"Elizabeth," Aunt Nan said sternly, "your mom needs to spend some time with adults. Perhaps this is something you need to pray about."

"Maybe he'll take you to Burger King, Mom. Mr. Hamilton took us there after a game once. He likes it," said Mike.

They were ganging up on her. Elizabeth crossed the porch and went inside. Maybe she should pray. The trouble was, she didn't know whether she should pray for God to help her accept Mr. Hamilton like she knew Aunt Nan meant, or whether she should pray for His help in figuring out a way to get rid of the man like she wanted to do.

Elizabeth felt a hollow place in the middle of her chest, cold and empty. Lonely.

Upstairs in her room, Elizabeth sat on the edge of her bed. I don't know what to do, God, she prayed in her mind. I don't even know what to pray. Things were never this mixed up when Dad was here. God, You don't want Mr. Hamilton to take Dad's place, do You?

Elizabeth drummed her fingers on top of the box of baseball cards as she tried to think of a way to get rid of Mr. Hamilton. Suddenly, she stopped and stared at the box. She saw the empty spaces and it hit her, leaving her breathless. Elizabeth realized she didn't have her purse or the Pete White card!

As she tried to think back to where she'd had it last, her mind went completely blank.

3
LOST AND FOUND AND LOST AGAIN

Elizabeth took a couple of deep breaths, closed her eyes, and asked God again to help her with this one. She felt a sense of calm as her prayer ended.

Still she couldn't stop the thoughts that pushed and shoved their way into her brain. Losing the card was like losing enough money to buy an entire wardrobe, even different shoes for each day of the week. It was like losing a little piece of her dad's short life. It meant big trouble if Mom found out.

Justin! Perhaps he'd remember what she'd done with her purse—and the card inside. She'd call him. Maybe not. She hated calling boys.

Elizabeth pulled the school directory out of her desk drawer. There was his name with the phone number right beside it. She touched the telephone beside her bed, then pulled her hand away like the receiver was hot. She closed the directory and stuck it in the drawer. 555-1409.

This was a good reason to call. It wasn't one of those, I-just-called-to-say-hi kind of things, Elizabeth thought. 555-1409. She grabbed the phone and punched the number in before she could think about it anymore.

Justin answered.

"Justin, it's me. Elizabeth." Even to her own ears, her voice sounded shaky. "I'm sorry to bother you, but I was wondering if you noticed my purse?"

"Your purse?"

"I left it someplace," Elizabeth said quickly.

"Oh! No, I don't know. When do you remember seeing it last?" he asked.

In her mind, Elizabeth walked back through the events of the afternoon. "At Mr. Becker's booth! During the photo session, he stuck it back behind the curtain so it wouldn't show in the picture." The scene appeared vividly. "Then I went to find Mom and forgot to get it." She fell back onto her bed.

"No problem then. I'm sure Mr. Becker has it, and we can get it in the morning when we go pick up the baseball card photos. You want to go with me?"

"Sure." Elizabeth sat back up. "The Pete White card was in there."

"No safer place for it," said Justin.

"I guess not. If that's where I left it." Elizabeth thought she remembered seeing it there last, but what if she'd left it someplace else.

"I'll come by after I finish my paper route, okay?"

"Great. See you then." Elizabeth hung up, feeling a little better. Maybe she'd left it in Mr. Hamilton's car. She could call him. His number was posted on the bulletin board in the kitchen. But if she called Mr. Hamilton, Mom would be sure to find out. It might be better if Mom didn't know anything until the card was safe and sound in the storage box.

The phone rang, and Elizabeth grabbed the receiver. Maybe someone had found her purse.

"Lydia?"

Elizabeth recognized Mr. Hamilton's voice. "No, it's Elizabeth."

"Is your mother there?"

Elizabeth made a quick decision. "No," she answered.

"I have a friend who called me a few minutes ago," said Mr. Hamilton, "and you won't believe what we talked about."

"Do you want to leave a message for Mom?" Elizabeth asked, knowing she was being rude.

"I'm getting to it," said Mr. Hamilton. "Eric is writing a book about Pete White."

Hearing the name was an unpleasant reminder that she'd lost the card.

"I told him about the baseball card you have, and it's the one he's looking for …"

"It's not for sale," Elizabeth interrupted.

Mr. Hamilton laughed. "He doesn't want to buy it. But he does want to see it and maybe use it in the book. Your name would be in there too, as the owner. Eric's done lots of research and thinks he knows what happened to Pete White."

In spite of herself, Elizabeth felt a tweak of curiosity. She'd always wanted to know why he'd disappeared.

"Eric will be in town tomorrow, and I want to bring him by to see the card. The book sounds great, doesn't it?"

"I'll check with Mom, and she'll call you back," said Elizabeth, knowing she wasn't going to do any such thing. Not only did she not want her mom talking to Mr. Hamilton, she definitely didn't want to get her started thinking about the baseball card.

"Thanks," said Mr. Hamilton.

"Wait!" Elizabeth practically shouted into the phone.

"I can hear just fine," he said.

"Did I leave a … a bag or anything in your car?" she asked.

"I didn't see it, but I'll check again if you want me to."

"No, that's okay. I'm pretty sure I know where it is."

"What kind of bag?" Mr. Hamilton asked.

"Just a bag," said Elizabeth. Anything she told him, Mom would be sure to find out.

"I'll see you soon, then," Mr. Hamilton said. "And if I find a *bag*, I'll drop it by your house."

"Thanks," said Elizabeth. She hung up.

Elizabeth knew it was going to be a long night. First thing the next morning she had to find out what happened to the card and her purse—before Mr. Hamilton had a chance to talk to Mom.

Bright and early the next morning, Elizabeth was out of bed and in the shower. She shampooed her hair, even though it could have gone one more day. She used perfumed soap rather than the regular shower soap. As she was drying off, there was a knock on the door.

"Sweetie, Justin is downstairs. He said the two of you were going to the baseball card shop?" Mom said as she stuck her head in the door.

Elizabeth jumped back and wrapped the towel around her body. "Justin is here? Already?"

Mom nodded. "I'll tell him you'll be down in a minute, okay?"

A minute! Elizabeth dried off most of the way, then combed the tangles out of her hair and waved the blow dryer over it. Would the card shop even be open?

Luckily she'd set her clothes out. Elizabeth dressed taking time only to make sure everything was on the right way and the right side out. She'd make her bed later.

Justin wasn't downstairs as she made her entrance. Had he gone without her? Elizabeth went into the kitchen. Mom sat at the table reading the paper and drinking a cup of coffee.

"Did he leave?"

"He's in front, playing catch with Mike," Mom said.

Elizabeth ran through the house, stopped at the front door, patted her hair down, and arranged her striped shirt.

"Justin!" she called out as she opened the door.

"Hi!" Justin tossed the ball back to Mike, then walked to the foot of the porch steps. "You ready?"

Elizabeth nodded.

"Where you going?" Mike asked.

"Baseball card shop," Elizabeth answered.

"I want to go," her brother said.

"No way."

"I have my own money. I want to get some Ozzie cards." Mike threw his glove down and ran up the steps. "Wait."

Mom appeared at the front door. "Where do you think you're going in such a hurry?" she asked Mike.

"To get my money so I can go with Justin and Elizabeth."

"I don't think so," said Mom. "You said you'd clean your room first thing this morning if you didn't have to do it last night."

"I will as soon as I get back," said Mike.

"Now." Mom pointed up the stairs. "You two go on," she said to Justin and Elizabeth.

"Mike, we can go some other time. Okay?" Justin said.

"Without Elizabeth?" he asked, pressing his

face against the screen and making a hideous face.

"Sure, just us guys."

Feeling a stab of guilt, Elizabeth knew she owed her mom for this one. She'd thank her as soon as she got her purse back.

"What did you think of the card show?" Justin asked.

"Pretty exciting. I had no idea baseball cards, any kind of cards like that, were such a big deal."

"I'm putting together a collection that I hope will pay my way through college. I've been collecting since I was about Mike's age, and I've got some good ones. Your Pete White would be a good card to add," Justin said, with a grin.

"I don't think so. I hope it's still in my purse." Elizabeth held up crossed fingers. And I hope I get it back before Mr. Hamilton and his friend show up to see it, she thought. Elizabeth lifted her hair off her neck. She should have pulled it back. Even though it was early, the sun was already hot, and they were walking fast.

The more they talked, the more comfortable Elizabeth felt. Justin was interested in lots of things, including books, one of her favorite subjects. They both loved mysteries and argued about who the best detectives were—the Hardy Boys or Nancy Drew. Elizabeth pointed out it took two boys to solve the same number of mysteries that Nancy solved by herself.

They reached the baseball card shop, and Justin held the door open, letting Elizabeth go in first.

"Hey, Jimbo!" Justin greeted the young man with long white-blond hair standing behind the counter at the card shop. "Mr. Becker here?"

"In the back. He has a *big* deal going down—he's set up an appearance by somebody, and he won't even tell *me* who it is."

"Do you know if the photos he took yesterday at the card show are ready?" Justin asked.

"And my purse. Does he have my purse?" Elizabeth added. "I think I left it in the dressing room at the card show."

"The cards are right here." Jim handed Justin a small manila envelope. "But I don't know anything about a purse. I'll check with Mr. Becker if you've got a minute."

Elizabeth nodded. Jim stuck his head behind a curtain that divided the front and back rooms. He said something, then Mr. Becker pulled the curtain open wide and looked right at Elizabeth. He shook his head and motioned for

Jim to go back to the front of the store. As soon as the younger man turned, the card dealer pulled the curtain closed.

"Sorry. He hasn't seen it."

Elizabeth felt her stomach take a dive. She'd been so sure. What was she going to tell Mom?

"It'll turn up," Justin said.

"I'll check some of the boxes he brought back that haven't been unpacked yet. It could have gotten stuck in one of them," said Jim.

"Thanks," Elizabeth said, hoping neither noticed her quivery voice. She wasn't about to let herself cry in front of Justin.

"C'mon. We'll go have a donut and look at these pictures." Justin held up the envelope. "Should be good for a laugh or two."

Elizabeth tried to smile.

"Later, Jim," Justin said.

Justin led Elizabeth to a small donut shop two doors down. He ordered two chocolate iced donuts, two vanilla iced, and two cartons of chocolate milk. "These are the best donuts I've ever eaten," he said, putting them down on a small round table.

Elizabeth sipped her milk, then took the donut Justin pushed toward her. It was delicious. She took another bite.

"Good, huh?" Justin smiled, donut crumbs all over his face. "Now for the unveiling." He wiped his hands on a napkin and opened the envelope. "These are great!"

He spread the three photos of her across the table. In the first, Elizabeth looked like she had just tasted something sour. She had to laugh. Quickly she covered it with her palm and slid it toward her side of the table.

"I hope you don't ever give me that look!" Justin teased. "But look at this one."

In the last picture they'd taken, Elizabeth looked not only like she knew what she was doing but like she was enjoying it.

"This one is mine." Justin tucked it back in the envelope.

Elizabeth couldn't believe he was keeping one of her pictures! Why? She didn't say anything for a minute, then remembered he hadn't shown his.

"Where are yours?" she asked, reaching for the envelope.

Justin held it in the air. "You don't want to see."

"I do! Fair is fair. You saw mine. C'mon." Elizabeth stood up and grabbed for the pictures. The envelope tipped, and they showered down on the table.

"Wow!" Elizabeth picked them up one by one. Justin had chosen a background and a uniform that made it look like an old card. In fact, he'd even posed like Pete White in one of the pictures. "This one is mine." She took the Pete White look-alike.

"You don't want one of those!" Justin protested.

"I may need it to replace the one I lost," Elizabeth said.

"We'll find your purse," Justin said confidently. "But I have a yard to mow today, and if I wait much longer, I'm going to roast."

Elizabeth pushed her chair away from the table.

"Are you going to Mike's game this week?" Justin asked.

"Maybe," she answered.

"I'll see you there." Justin took off in the opposite direction from her house.

Elizabeth walked along slowly, glancing down at Justin's photo every few steps. When she got to the corner of her street, she saw a familiar car, a black Volvo, driving toward her. Good, she'd missed Mr. Hamilton. He didn't seem to notice her as he drove past.

When she reached her house, Elizabeth started to go upstairs. Aunt Nan stopped her.

"Look what I found on the porch swing." Aunt Nan held Elizabeth's purse by the strap, swinging it back and forth.

Elizabeth grabbed it and hugged it.

"Not a very responsible thing to do." Aunt Nan pointed her finger at Elizabeth.

"I didn't leave it out here," Elizabeth said. "Mr. Hamilton! I left it in Mr. Hamilton's car, and he must have found it and dropped it off."

"When?" Aunt Nan looked puzzled.

"This morning. I saw him as I was turning the corner."

"Wonder why he didn't knock?" asked Aunt Nan. "Mike!"

Mike's face appeared at the top of the stairs.

"Did you talk to Mr. Hamilton today?" Aunt Nan asked.

"No, is he here?" He started down.

"Get back up there and clean your room. He is not here." Aunt Nan turned back to Elizabeth. "Doesn't matter. You got the purse back."

"Where's Mom?" Elizabeth asked.

"Went to the market to get some things for both of us." Aunt Nan wandered back to the kitchen.

Elizabeth ran up the stairs and into her room, closing the door behind her. She opened her purse and dug around, finally finding the cool plastic of the card case. Pete White was safe at home.

Anxious to tell Justin, she dialed the phone and got a busy signal. Two faces stared up at her from the rumpled sheets—Justin in a navy blue baseball cap with a red cardinal and Pete White with the same cap. It was amazing how authentic Justin's card looked, even next to the real thing. She picked the two cards up to look at them a little closer. The room got cold, like someone had turned the air conditioning up to the max and aimed it right at her.

Memory could play funny tricks, she thought. The Pete White card didn't seem the same as it had been before. She couldn't quite put her finger on it, but it was different.

Elizabeth's conscience nagged at her. She had the card back, maybe she should tell Mom about Mr. Hamilton's call. He probably hadn't knocked because he'd thought Mom didn't want to talk to him. And wouldn't that be awful? She couldn't stop the grin that spread across her face.

4

PETE WHITE IS COMING TO TOWN?

The door to her room flew open. Elizabeth tucked the cards under the covers of the bed.

"Look! A picture of me and Ozzie Smith!" Mike jumped on her bed and held up a snapshot.

"Where'd you get that?" Elizabeth asked, leaning forward to look.

"From Mr. Hamilton. He took it at the card show yesterday." The photo had a border, just like the one around the baseball card Mr. Becker had made of her. "Give me that." Elizabeth examined it closely. It was exactly like her card. She tapped it against her chin, thinking.

"Elizabeth?"

"Here, take your card." She handed it back to Mike.

"What's the matter?"

"Nothing. Who said you could come in my room?" Elizabeth wanted him out so she could think some more. Mr. Hamilton had stopped by the house, but he hadn't bothered to talk to anyone. He'd also somehow had a baseball card made. She wanted to look at the Pete White card again. Elizabeth had a sinking feeling about it.

"Don't you like my picture?" Mike looked like he was going to cry.

"I like it." Elizabeth reached out and gave her brother a hug. "Now you have a picture to hang beside your autograph. You're so lucky."

"We're lucky that Mr. Hamilton likes Mom."

No one in her family was going to listen to anything bad she had to say about Mr. Hamilton; Elizabeth was sure of that. Who would listen? Would Justin? He seemed to like Mr. Hamilton almost as much as Mike did.

The telephone rang. Elizabeth answered.

"Elizabeth, ..."

"Meghan! I have so much to tell you." Elizabeth felt better hearing her friend's voice. Meghan would listen to her.

"I can't talk right now. I need to know if your mom can give me a ride to dance class tomorrow. We'll give you a ride home," said Meghan.

"I'm sure she would. Just a minute." Elizabeth covered the mouthpiece. "Mike, go on. I want to talk to Meghan."

Mike backed out of the room, staring down at the photo.

"All the way gone," Elizabeth called when she didn't hear him go down the steps.

"You won't believe what's happening here," Elizabeth said to Meghan.

"I really can't talk," Meghan said. "I have an orthodontist appointment, and we're already late. Can you give me the quick version?"

"I went to a baseball card show with Justin Thayer!"

Meghan practically screamed into her ear. "You didn't!"

"He's Mike's baseball coach. But my mom had a sort of date too."

"Who with?"

"Mr. Hamilton, Mike's other baseball coach."

"He's a teacher at the high school. My sister had him for photography, and she had the biggest crush on him. For a teacher, he's a hunk! Aren't you excited?"

"Not about Mr. Hamilton. Meghan, I think he …"

"All right, Mom. I'm coming. I have to go, Elizabeth. Save all the gory details for tomorrow, okay? Bye-bye!" The phone clicked.

Elizabeth stared at the silent receiver, then hung it up.

"Elizabeth! Justin's here again!" Mom called. She wondered how long Mom had been home.

Halfway down the steps, Elizabeth heard a chorus of excited voices coming from the front porch. Her palms started to sweat. She heard Justin say something about Pete White, then a voice she recognized as Mr. Hamilton's cut him off. Elizabeth was sure Mom was out there too, and all this talk about Pete White was making her very nervous. Surely Justin wouldn't mention that she'd taken the card to the show. The only way she'd find out what was going on was to go outside. Elizabeth took a deep breath.

"Hi," she said as she pushed the screen door open.

Justin turned and grabbed her arm. "You won't believe this. You just won't believe it!" His face was flushed, and his hair stuck out at odd angles.

Elizabeth glanced toward Mr. Hamilton. He sat on the swing alongside a man she'd never seen. Mom was leaning against the porch railing. They were all looking at her and Justin.

"Pete White!" Justin said. "He's coming here."

"To our house?" Elizabeth stared at Justin.

The adults laughed.

Elizabeth felt herself blush.

Justin shook his head. He wiped his forehead with the back of his free hand. "To Mr. Becker's card shop. That's what he was working on this morning. I stopped by after I finished my lawn to see if ..." He stopped.

Elizabeth shook her head slightly.

"Well, anyway, he had a poster up with a picture of Pete White, the same picture as your baseball card. It said he'd be at the shop on Saturday. And it only costs $25 to meet him."

The man sitting next to Mr. Hamilton was chewing on his lower lip. He shook his head, then turned to Mr. Hamilton.

"I don't understand. I was so sure ..."

"Elizabeth, this is Don, ... er ... Mr. Hamilton's friend, Eric Sommers. He's the one who's writing the book about Pete White. The one you forgot to tell me about," said Mom.

"Nice to meet you, Mr. Sommers," Elizabeth said.

Mr. Sommers ignored her, continuing to direct his comments to Mr. Hamilton. "The timing of this whole thing is incredible. I mean, for me to be here just when this so-called Pete White shows up."

"The timing couldn't be better for Mr. Becker either," said Justin. "Jim told me that Mr. Becker had been talking about closing the shop because he couldn't afford to keep it open. But Jim said this will put the shop on the map."

"If he pulls it off," said Mr. Sommers.

"What do you mean?" Justin asked.

"I've done a lot of investigating for my book, and I'm surprised that this Becker fellow has turned up Pete White."

"You don't think Pete White is really coming?" asked Justin.

Mr. Sommers sighed. "I don't know if the man who is coming is really Pete White."

"Are you calling Mr. Becker a liar?" Justin took a step toward the swing.

"Justin," Mr. Hamilton's voice held a note of warning. "I think Eric doesn't know what to make of this development."

"Elizabeth, go get your dad's baseball card," Mom said. "And I'll get some lemonade for all of us. It's awfully hot out here."

Elizabeth followed Mom into the cool darkness of the house. She ran upstairs and got the card. She still couldn't shake the feeling something was wrong with it.

When she returned, Mr. Hamilton and Mr.

Sommers were talking in low tones. Elizabeth noticed Mr. Sommers was doing most of the talking. She handed the card to Mr. Hamilton.

"Thanks for bringing my purse back," Elizabeth said.

"Your purse?" Mr. Hamilton had a blank look on his face.

"When you dropped off Mike's picture. I saw you driving away," said Elizabeth.

"I did drive by, but when your mother's car wasn't in the drive, I went on. I ran into her at the grocery store and gave her the picture then."

"Then how did my purse get on the swing?" Elizabeth asked.

"Perhaps you left it there," Mom said from the doorway.

"I didn't. I didn't have it last night when we got home from the card show."

"You didn't say a word about it then," said Mom. She passed a tray of lemonade around the porch.

Mr. Hamilton handed the card to Mr. Sommers. "This is the same card I had when we were kids," he said. "Remember?"

Mr. Sommers peered closely at the card. He shook his head. "This isn't the same card you had," he said. "This card is a fake."

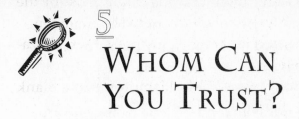

5
WHOM CAN
YOU TRUST?

Elizabeth felt like someone had hit her in the stomach.

Mom and Mr. Hamilton both moved closer to Mr. Sommers.

"Pete White had blue eyes," Elizabeth heard Mr. Sommers say. *That* was what was wrong with the card.

"Poor, Michael," Mom said. "He was so proud of this card." That made Elizabeth feel even worse. Her dad's card had been the real thing. If she hadn't disobeyed Mom, it still would be. It was her fault that the real card had been replaced with a fake by ...

Elizabeth watched Mr. Hamilton. He was saying and doing all the right things—shaking his head like he couldn't believe it, consoling Mom. Elizabeth wanted to shout out her accusation, but she managed to stay quiet. She didn't know how she'd do it, but she was going to show everyone the truth about Mr. Hamilton.

He'd said how much he wanted her card, and he'd had her purse and the card overnight. He obviously knew how to make baseball cards because he'd made one for Mike. And what had Meghan said? He taught photography! It all added up.

"I guess I won't be able to use this in my book after all. If there is a book." Mr. Sommers stared at the porch floor. This was turning out to be a cheery party, thought Elizabeth.

"I can't believe they were counterfeiting baseball cards even in the 1950s," said Justin. He'd finally gotten his hands on the Pete White card and was checking it carefully. "From all I've read, the reason it's so common today is because the equipment is so available."

Mr. Sommers' head snapped up. "He's right. They didn't have the technology then."

"But this card hasn't been anyplace but in this box for years and years," said Mom.

Elizabeth sank to the porch steps under the weight of the guilt. She was amazed at how innocent Mr. Hamilton continued to look and act. How did he do it?

"Think you could take me by that card shop? The one where Pete White supposedly is going to appear?" Mr. Sommers asked.

"We can stop by Becker's on our way back to my house," said Mr. Hamilton.

"Justin, by the way, I think I have a little surprise for the team. Remember that tournament at the lake? The one that would have cost us about $175 in registration fees plus transportation? I got the money and just in time. The deadline is tomorrow," said Mr. Hamilton. "You'll be able to go, won't you?"

"You bet!" Justin answered excitedly. "Are we still going to camp out one night?"

"Marshmallows, hot dogs, the whole show."

"You're a brave man—camping with 12 six-year-olds," Mom smiled.

"Yes," Mr. Hamilton laughed.

"You get a sponsor?" Justin asked.

"Sponsor?"

"To pay the entry fee," said Justin.

"Yeah, right. I did," said Mr. Hamilton.

"Mike's going to be so excited," said Mom. "His first campout."

"Mark it on your calendar," Mr. Hamilton said to Justin. "I don't want to end up by myself with the team."

You may not have to worry about that, Elizabeth thought, watching Mr. Hamilton and Mr.

Sommers get up to leave. Mom and Justin waved as the two men drove away.

"Don't worry so much about that card," Mom said, putting her hand on Elizabeth's shoulder. "At least Dad never knew."

Small consolation, Elizabeth thought.

"Want some more lemonade?" Mom asked.

"No," Elizabeth answered.

"No, thanks," said Justin. He sat down on the steps beside Elizabeth.

"I have to go to the pool to pick up Mike in a few minutes," said Mom. "I may stop and get some sandwiches at the deli. It's too hot to cook."

"Veggie for me," said Elizabeth, although she wasn't sure she could eat anything.

Justin and Elizabeth sat in silence. Justin turned the Pete White card over and over.

"I wonder why Mr. Becker didn't say anything about the card being a fake?" he finally said.

"Justin, don't you know?" Elizabeth had hoped he'd figured out the same thing she had.

"Know what?"

Elizabeth looked at him and could tell from the expression on his face that Justin didn't have a clue.

"The card was *real* when Mr. Becker saw it," said Elizabeth.

Justin looked confused.

"Mr. Hamilton replaced the real card with the fake one when he took it out of my purse— the purse that I left in his car."

"That's crazy!" Justin stood up. He paced back and forth across the porch.

"Is not. He made a baseball card for Mike, so he knows how."

"So does Mr. Becker. So do lots of people," said Justin.

"But Mr. Hamilton was the one who had the chance to take the card," said Elizabeth. "And he said he wanted it."

"You believe that a man who would bring your little brother baseball cards and take a bunch of little kids on a campout would steal a baseball card?" Justin moved to sit in the swing, leaning back and crossing his arms.

"He's trying to *buy* Mike and it's working— on my brother *and* my mother."

"I'd like it if he'd take my mother out. You should see some of the guys she dates," said Justin. "Consider yourself lucky."

Elizabeth didn't even know that Justin didn't live with both his parents. "Maybe you should invite your mom to the games."

"I don't think he'd even notice. Haven't you seen the way he looks at your mom?" Justin said.

Elizabeth had, but she didn't know that everyone else had too. "Back to the point. If Mr. Hamilton or Mr. Becker didn't take the card, then who did? You were the only other person who knew about the baseball card," said Elizabeth.

Justin shot off the swing, leaving it swaying wildly. "Now it's me! Elizabeth, get a grip. If that's what you think of me ..."

Elizabeth reached out to steady the swing. "No, I didn't mean ..."

"I'm not sure what you mean, but when you figure it out, call me." Justin jumped off the porch, cut across the yard, and was out of sight before Elizabeth could stop him.

6
THE MYSTERY
GETS SMELLIER
AND SMELLIER

"Don't worry, Mrs. Bryan. My mom will pick us up," Meghan assured Elizabeth's mom as they climbed out of the car.

"I don't want you two walking home alone in the dark," Mom said.

"It's not dark when we finish dancing, but we won't walk home alone, I promise." Elizabeth slammed the car door. She had no intention of riding home with Meghan, but as long as she arrived home before dark, Mom would never know.

"I thought we would never get here!" Meghan said. "Now, tell me, tell me everything."

"What?"

"About Justin Thayer! This is so incredible. You actually went on a date with a boy!"

"It wasn't a date," Elizabeth protested. "He

was invited to go to the same place by the same person who invited me, so we went together."

"So, how was it?"

The two of them sat on the bench along one wall of the dance studio and changed into ballet shoes. Elizabeth immediately sat on the floor and started stretching. Meghan sank down beside her with a groan.

"How do you do that? Touch your nose to your knee?"

"Keep working on it. You'll get there." Elizabeth wished she'd never mentioned Justin to Meghan, not after what had happened yesterday.

"So you went to this baseball thing. Did you have fun?"

"It was fun. We had our pictures taken and made into baseball cards."

"Do you have them with you? Let me see?"

The class ahead of them was still on the floor. Miss Karen gave them a dirty look.

"Shhh! No, I don't have it with me, but I do have one," said Elizabeth.

"Are you going out again? When?" Meghan was full of questions.

"I don't know. We had kind of a fight," Elizabeth said. She wished she had time to explain to Meghan about the counterfeit baseball card and her suspicions. Meghan would believe her, she was sure.

"A fight! Already. This is getting better and better."

"Girls! To the barre. Vite! Vite!" Miss Karen called out.

Meghan let out another groan. "Head high, shoulders back, tummy in, bottom under. Who can do this stuff?" she whispered.

They took their places at opposite ends of the barre, and Elizabeth, for the first time in two days, forgot about her problems with the baseball card.

Class passed quickly and Elizabeth, as always, was sorry when it ended. She took two hours of dance every week, ballet on Tuesday with Meghan and tap on Thursday with her mother. She decided she'd tell Miss Karen they might miss Thursday.

Meghan was ready to leave by the time Elizabeth finished her conversation with the teacher. "You go ahead," Elizabeth told her. "I'm going to stay and work on turns with Miss Karen."

"I promised your mom we'd bring you home," said Meghan.

"I'll call her, and she'll come pick me up.

She won't mind. And if she's busy, Aunt Nan can come."

"Are you sure?"

"I'm sure. I'm so frustrated with that one turn."

"Yeah, yeah. I can't do any of them without getting so dizzy I almost fall down," said Meghan.

"You need to learn to spot."

"So they say, so they say. You be sure to call me tomorrow. I still don't know everything I want to know about you and Justin."

"I will. I'll call tomorrow," Elizabeth promised.

"Not before 9 or 9:30."

"Of course not. You need your beauty sleep."

Meghan stuck her tongue out at Elizabeth as she left the studio.

Elizabeth waited to make sure her friend was out of sight, then quickly slipped out the door. She wanted to go by the card shop and look at the Pete White poster herself. Maybe she could even get Mr. Becker to tell her how someone went about counterfeiting a card. The thing that bothered her was why were Pete White's eyes brown on her fake card?

The dance studio was almost directly behind the baseball card shop. Elizabeth decided it would be quicker to cut between two buildings to the alley between the studio and the shop than to walk around the block.

In the alley, Elizabeth paused and tried to pick out which building housed the card shop. From the back, all the stores looked the same. She finally decided it was the one with the dumpster blocking the space between the two buildings—the space she needed to cut through to get to the front of the shop. On second glance, Elizabeth thought perhaps there was a small opening between the dumpster and the wall that she'd fit through.

Looking over her shoulder, Elizabeth ran to the dumpster and tried to squeeze herself through the small opening. It was too tight. She dropped her dance bag and tried to move the dumpster enough to be able to fit through. When it finally moved, it made a high-pitched, screeching noise, and Elizabeth stopped immediately. She decided she'd better take the long way around.

When Elizabeth reached down to get her bag, she caught a glimpse of a brightly colored piece of paper. Something about it seemed familiar. She picked it up.

Elizabeth gasped. She was face to face with a bad copy of the Pete White baseball card. This one was washed out—the colors pale and the details hazy. No one would ever take it for the real thing. She squinted—the eyes were *blue* in this one. What was it doing in the alley behind Becker's Card Shop? Maybe if Justin could see this …

Elizabeth heard the back door of the shop open. She froze, clutching the baseball card to her chest. Through the open door she heard a burst of laughter, men's laughter.

Elizabeth didn't want anybody to see her with the card. She wasn't sure whom she could trust at this point.

Looking right, then left, Elizabeth frantically searched for a place to hide. With the exception of the dumpster, the alley was completely bare. Help me, God, she breathed. I'm really stuck this time.

Taking a deep breath, Elizabeth jumped up and grabbed the edge of the dumpster pulling herself up and over the edge. She closed the lid over her head.

7
FALLEN HEROES

Inside the dumpster, Elizabeth found herself crouching on a floor covered with paper and cardboard boxes and, to her relief, nothing squishy. She continued to hold her breath, but finally she had to let it out. She breathed in quickly and shallowly. Elizabeth had to put her hand over her mouth to keep from coughing. The smell, even when she wasn't breathing, seemed to seep through her clothes and into the pores of her skin. She could almost taste it. Immediately, Elizabeth began to sweat. Not only was her hiding place smelly—it was hot.

Very cautiously, Elizabeth raised the lid of the dumpster enough to let some air inside. It wasn't much better, but a little clear air moved over her, and the smells were slightly diluted. She could barely hear two male voices, talking on and on.

Elizabeth twisted her head to try and hear. The words were still fuzzy, but she clearly recognized the voices of the speakers and almost dropped the lid. What business could Mr.

Hamilton possibly have with Mr. Becker? What she needed right now was a deep, deep breath, but there was no way to take one from inside the dumpster. Elizabeth closed her eyes and willed herself to calm down.

Sounds that she knew were words floated over the dumpster. If only Elizabeth could figure a way to invite them inside. She thought she heard *team*, then *card*, perhaps *Musial*, but she wasn't sure of anything. She tried to see what was happening, but there was no way without lifting the lid higher and possibly giving away her hideout.

Finally, Elizabeth heard the door shut, then the sound of footsteps. When they seemed to stop momentarily beside the dumpster, she held her breath again, afraid to make even the slightest move. The footsteps started again, moving past the dumpster, then gradually getting softer and softer until she couldn't hear anything.

Elizabeth still waited, wanting nothing more than to escape but fearing that someone lurked outside the dumpster waiting for her to pop out. Was Mr. Hamilton trying to sell her Pete White card to Mr. Becker? Had he already sold it to him, and had Mr. Becker make a copy of it so she wouldn't know it was gone? Elizabeth knew there was also a chance that Mr. Becker had taken her card and replaced it with a copy. But she'd seen Mr. Hamilton on her street just when the purse was returned. He still seemed like the number one suspect to her.

Slowly, Elizabeth opened the lid and peeked over the edge of the dumpster. No one was in sight. She propped the dumpster cover back into the same position it had been in before her dip inside, then climbed out.

If only there was someone she could discuss this whole mess with! If she tried to say anything to Mom or Aunt Nan about Mr. Hamilton, they wouldn't listen. And Justin wouldn't listen to anything bad about either Mr. Becker or Mr. Hamilton. It seemed to Elizabeth she was turning out to be the bad guy in a situation where she felt like the victim.

The odor of the dumpster clung to her clothes. Elizabeth sniffed her T-shirt and wondered how she was going to explain to Mom how it had gotten so smelly.

Elizabeth decided to abandon her plan to visit the card shop. Mr. Becker was one of the last people she wanted to see right now.

As she started to leave the alley, Elizabeth's foot caught on something and she stumbled. She bumped into the dumpster, stopping her fall but causing a terrible clang. She stayed down, hoping no one would come out to see what was going on.

When there was no sign of movement, Elizabeth used her toes to investigate the bundle she'd tripped over. Her breath caught.

It was her dance bag, bright pink with her name spelled out in shiny silver letters for anyone to see. Elizabeth silently reassured herself. No one saw it, besides there were jillions of Elizabeth's in the world. Who would think it was her? But what if someone had seen it and realized it was her?

Elizabeth slung the bag over her shoulder and walked quickly to the end of the alley, then turned toward home. As she walked past her church, she slowed. Perhaps Pastor James would talk to her. She started up the walk, but the church was dark and silent. Elizabeth closed her eyes and whispered a prayer asking God for some help. Taking a deep breath, she realized she wasn't alone after all. God had helped her through her dad's death. He wouldn't desert her now.

When Elizabeth opened her eyes, Justin was pedaling her way on his bicycle!

"Justin," Elizabeth called, but not very

loudly. When he didn't look her way, she yelled.

Justin stopped. He hesitated a moment, then walked the bike to meet her.

"Do you have a minute?" Elizabeth asked.

"I guess. What now?"

"Come over here and sit down. I have something to show you." She sat down on a concrete bench under a tree in the church yard.

"I think what I said to you, you know, earlier," Justin began. "Well, it was probably really uncool because I know you're upset about the card and everything."

"That's what I want to talk about. First, I never, never thought you took anything. Okay?"

Justin nodded.

"But, I do think somebody did."

Justin sighed and looked away.

"Wait a minute. Look at this." She handed him the card she'd found outside the dumpster.

"What is it?" Justin glanced at it, then took a longer look. "What *is* it? Where'd you get it?"

"You have to listen and not go all ballistic on me, okay?" said Elizabeth. She waited.

"I'm listening," Justin said impatiently.

"Okay, I'm just going to tell it like it happened, with no comments on what I think about it. I was going to the baseball card shop so I could take a look at that poster you said was like my baseball card and see if Pete White had blue or brown eyes. I also wanted someone to maybe explain how cards are counterfeited. I was coming from dance lessons and the studio is right behind the card shop, so I cut through the alley. There was this dumpster blocking the space between the buildings and when I went up to it, there was this card, this definitely-not-real Pete White card, on the ground beside the dumpster.

"I was just standing there staring at it when I heard somebody coming from the shop, so I climbed into the dumpster and closed the lid."

"You what?" Justin burst out laughing.

Elizabeth felt her cheeks burn.

"That must be what I smell." He laughed some more.

Elizabeth scooted back away from Justin a little. She smelled. How embarrassing!

"Anyway, I couldn't breathe inside the dumpster because it was so hot and stinky, so I lifted the lid just a little. You won't believe who was out there talking. Mr. Becker—"

"It's Mr. Becker's shop," Justin interrupted.

"But he was talking to Mr. Hamilton. When they finished, I climbed out of the dumpster and started home. Then I met you." Elizabeth waited for Justin to say something.

He took his baseball hat off, rubbed his hands through his hair, then put the hat back on. Justin looked at the card a little longer.

"Where do you suppose that card came from?" Elizabeth asked.

"It's a copy," Justin said.

"I agree. But it has blue eyes, and it was in Mr. Becker's dumpster."

"Were there any other cards like this in there? Maybe he makes photocopies for record purposes," said Justin.

"I didn't check," said Elizabeth, realizing too late it would have been a good thing to do.

"How do you think it got there?" Justin finally asked.

"I'm so confused I don't know what to think," Elizabeth admitted.

"You were so sure Mr. Hamilton had switched your real Pete White card with a fake. Do you still think that?" Justin asked.

"He could have. He knows a lot about cameras. My friend Meghan said so. Her sister had him for a photography teacher in high school. He could have thrown this one in Mr. Becker's dumpster thinking no one would think it was strange to find a baseball card in there."

"But it's not the same as your card. This one has blue eyes."

The eyes again. "I'm sure my dad's real card had blue eyes too. I knew something was wrong with that new one as soon as I saw it. I just couldn't figure out what."

"It's so strange. If someone was going to make a fake, why would they make such a mistake? You know, the eyes?" asked Justin.

Elizabeth knew then that Justin was starting to listen to what she had to say.

"Maybe Mr. Becker made the fake card and switched it. I didn't actually see Mr. Hamilton bring my purse back," said Elizabeth. "Mr. Becker has all that equipment to make cards."

"True."

"Or they could be working together."

Justin sighed again, long and loud.

"I know you like both of them a lot," Elizabeth said, wishing she wasn't the one who had put the sad expression on his face.

"What should we do now?" asked Justin.

"I was hoping you'd know," Elizabeth said, smiling and feeling a sense of relief that she had another helper to solve this puzzle.

8

CLOSE CALL

"The first thing we should do is go back to Mr. Becker's dumpster and see if there are any more cards like this," Elizabeth said. "And I still haven't seen that poster."

Justin nodded.

"The thing is," Elizabeth continued, "I'm late, and I'm going to get in big trouble if I don't get home really soon. If my mom finds out that I walked home instead of getting a ride, I'm going to be in trouble." Elizabeth chewed on her lower lip, trying to figure a way out of this mess.

"Would she be mad if I walked with you?" Justin asked.

The suggestion caught Elizabeth off guard. She stared at him, caught herself, then shrugged. "She wouldn't be *as* mad. As long as I wasn't out walking by myself. My mom's like that sometimes, kind of overprotective." Elizabeth didn't know if the warmth she was feeling was from embarrassment or from Justin offering to walk her home.

"All moms are," Justin answered, grinning. "We'll do a quick run through the alley first to see if we can find anything else like this." He held up the card.

They circled back to the end of the block and entered the alley. The sound of Justin's bicycle rolling along seemed almost deafening to Elizabeth in the silence. The buildings buffered any sound from passing cars and kept out any light cast by the street lamps.

"I found the card right there," Elizabeth whispered, pointing to a spot on the ground.

Justin leaned his bicycle against the wall, then dropped to his hands and knees to look on the ground. Elizabeth squatted beside him, keeping her eye on the door to the shop.

"Maybe I should check inside the dumpster," said Justin.

"Then you'll smell like me," Elizabeth said.

"Do you want to go inside again?"

Elizabeth shook her head.

Justin climbed easily over the side and dropped into the trash bin. Elizabeth watched as he sifted through the layers of trash in the bottom of the dumpster.

"Take this." He handed her a scrap of paper. "And this."

Elizabeth had her hand on the paper when the door opened and Mr. Becker backed out, stopping to lock the shop. Elizabeth let go of the evidence and motioned for Justin to stay down. She pressed herself against the wall and hoped the shop owner would go the other way.

Mr. Becker almost walked right by her. When he did see her, his hands flew up in front of his face, almost as if he thought Elizabeth was going to attack him. "Whaa … You almost scared me to death," the man said.

Elizabeth saw his Adam's apple bob up and down as he swallowed rapidly. "Sorry." She stared at the ground, moving her foot back and forth in front of her, watching the pattern it made in the dust.

"So what are you doing hanging around back here?" Mr. Becker looked around quickly.

"I was at dance class and decided to take a shortcut. This dumpster was blocking the way," said Elizabeth. She quickly wondered how many lies God would forgive her for telling. She was certainly racking up a lot in one day.

"I see." Mr. Becker looked at her closely.

Elizabeth squirmed. She didn't like being inspected.

"Don't I know you?" His eyes got big and his mouth dropped open. "Justin's friend!" he said.

"I was also thinking about buying my little brother some baseball cards, for his birthday. It's coming up. I know he'd like something with Ozzie Smith on it." Elizabeth was anxious to get Mr. Becker out of the alley before he discovered Justin in his dumpster.

"You'll have to come back tomorrow. Well, maybe not tomorrow. I'm having kind of a special event in the shop this week, and you wouldn't be interested. Next week. Come back then."

"You mean Pete White? But I am interested!" Elizabeth couldn't believe she'd brought it up. The words popped out of her mouth before she could stop them.

Mr. Becker took a step toward her. He frowned. "Who told you about that?"

"I just heard," said Elizabeth.

"Means your card won't be so rare after all. You'll be lucky to get a hundred dollars for it." Mr. Becker looked at his watch. "Need a lift home?"

"No, thank you." Elizabeth's hand lighted

on the handlebars of Justin's bike. "I'm riding." She put the bike between her and Mr. Becker.

"Suit yourself. Kind of late for you to be out ... alone."

Elizabeth threw her leg over the bar and rode away from Mr. Becker. He made her skin crawl like it was a size too small for her.

At the end of the alley, Elizabeth turned toward home. As soon as she was out of sight, she jumped off the bicycle and leaned against the brick building. She couldn't believe how close they'd come to getting caught.

It wasn't long before Elizabeth heard footsteps running down the alley. Justin burst around the corner and stopped. He checked his bicycle, then turned to her.

"I thought we were dead!" the two of them said at the same time.

At that, they burst into laughter, leaving Elizabeth so weak, she had to sit down on the curb.

"Why did you have to mention Pete White?" Justin asked.

"I don't know. It just came out."

"A hundred dollars. I know guys who said their dads would spend a thousand dollars to have a Pete White card," said Justin.

"A thousand dollars! For a baseball card?"

"I read it on a computer bulletin board."

"What's that?" asked Elizabeth.

"You dial a number with your computer modem, and it hooks you up with a lot of people talking about stuff you're interested in. There's a local bulletin board for guys interested in baseball cards," Justin explained.

"Guys? Just guys use this bulletin board?"

"Maybe girls. I don't know. People don't use their real names. I sign on as ..." Justin's voice trailed off.

"What?"

"It's too dumb."

"Tell me anyway," said Elizabeth.

"Batting A. Thousand."

"What?"

Justin groaned. "See you don't even get it."

Silence built up between them. Elizabeth kept trying to figure out what the name meant. She didn't want to have to ask Mike.

"In baseball, hitting the ball once every three times up to bat is good," Justin finally said. "Batting a thousand means hitting the ball every time. Nobody does it."

"Not even Pete White?" asked Elizabeth. Dad had said he was a good hitter.

"Not even anybody ever," said Justin.

"Oh." Elizabeth thought she had to say something. She suddenly remembered. "What about those pieces of paper in the dumpster?"

"When you dropped them back inside, I couldn't find them again because the light was so bad."

"What were they?" she asked.

"I couldn't really tell, but they were the same size as a baseball card, and they felt like baseball cards. Why would somebody in the business of selling baseball cards throw away a perfectly good card?" Justin asked.

"Maybe we should go back," said Elizabeth.

"I wish we had a flashlight."

Elizabeth realized that it was almost dark. She jumped up. "I'd better get home and fast." She walked to the corner.

Justin wheeled his bike after her. "What about tomorrow evening? About this time? I have to play in a baseball game at 5 o'clock. You could come and watch it, then tell your mom that we're going out for a soda or something. I'll bring a flashlight and maybe we'll be able to see what we find."

"Only if we're sure that Mr. Becker is nowhere around!" said Elizabeth.

"Very sure," Justin echoed.

2
RED LIGHT
MEANS
ANSWERS

Elizabeth sat alone on the highest bleacher, trying to figure out what was happening on the field below her. Justin had turned around once and looked right at her but hadn't even waved. She wondered if she should have come at all. Her backpack, holding a flashlight and a magnifying glass, lay beneath her feet. She wasn't sure why she'd brought the magnifying glass, but it had seemed like a good idea at the time.

"We meet again."

Elizabeth looked over at the man who had parked himself next to her. Her skin shrunk up at the sight of Mr. Becker, just as it had done after their conversation the night before. She placed her feet firmly on top of her backpack.

"Do you think you could give me a special deal on a ticket to see Pete White?" Elizabeth said, then clapped her hand over her mouth.

"I might, I might. And I just might let you in on a little secret. White is bringing a card along that I'm raffling off during his visit. How many chances can I sell you?" asked Mr. Becker, looking slightly amused.

"You have a Pete White card?" Odd, thought Elizabeth, right after a visit with Mr. Hamilton.

"So you're here to watch Justin play?"

"Why are you here?" Elizabeth asked.

"I asked you first," said Mr. Becker.

"I'm here to watch Justin."

"I am too. Plus a few of my other customers. I also had to take some pictures of a team that's playing in the next game. Can't make a living from baseball cards alone." Mr. Becker patted a large, black bag that he'd set between them.

I'll bet you can't, Elizabeth thought. Although with a few more finds like the Pete White card you may be able to make a pretty good living.

"Your dad asked me to take pictures of your little brother's team too," said Mr. Becker.

"My dad?"

"He coaches the Astros, right?"

"That's NOT my dad," Elizabeth informed him.

"Sorry. He was with you and your mother and brother at the card show. I thought ..."

"You thought wrong." How many other people had the same idea about Mr. Hamilton? Elizabeth wondered. It had happened just as she'd feared. Had he said he was her dad when he sold the baseball card?

Mr. Becker let out a shrill whistle, almost bursting Elizabeth's eardrum. "Good play!" he yelled.

She quickly looked at the field and saw Justin running toward the bench with the rest of his team. He picked up a bat, carried it out to a white circle drawn in the dust, and started swinging it around.

"Justin is a pretty good hitter. And he's a great fielder. That play he just made. Wow!" Mr. Becker clapped his hands a few times, then yelled, "Wait for a good one. You're a hitter!"

Elizabeth sat forward, her eyes following Justin as he walked to the plate and got into position. The pitcher threw the ball.

"Strike one!" the umpire yelled.

Elizabeth tensed. That wasn't a good start. Her palms started to feel moist and hot. She rubbed them on her shorts.

The pitcher threw again.

"Strike two!"

Sweat popped out above Elizabeth's lip. She wiped it off, then started chewing on her thumbnail even though she'd vowed to stop.

The ball came toward Justin and he swung. At the sound of the bat connecting with the ball, Elizabeth jumped out of her seat and started yelling, "Go! Go! Run!" She clapped her hands until they stung.

Justin made it all the way to third base.

"Told you he could hit," said Mr. Becker. He picked up his black bag and slung the strap over his shoulder. "I think I'm going to go home early for a change. Be sure to stop by sometime soon to get those cards for your brother. I have something I think he'll like."

Elizabeth hardly noticed that Mr. Becker had gone. The next batter struck out, but the one after that hit the ball again and Justin ran across the plate. She could have sworn he looked straight at her as he ran back to the bench.

Justin's team won the game 1-0. Elizabeth wasn't sure what she should do when the game ended. She moved from the top of the bleachers down to the first row and waited. She watched as Justin drank a bottle of Gatorade with the rest of his team and talked to the coach. He slowly packed his equipment into a gym bag, then scanned the bleachers. She lifted her hand and wiggled her fingers in a shy wave.

"Did you like the game?" Justin asked.

"It was exciting," Elizabeth answered. "You played great!"

"Thanks." Justin looked around at the crowd. "You still want to go get something to drink?"

"You just had something. I'm okay. And Justin, Mr. Becker isn't at the shop. He was here and said he was going home."

"I thought I saw him sitting with you."

"It's kind of weird, how he keeps turning up everywhere we are lately." Elizabeth shivered.

"He's always at these games," said Justin.

"Do you have your bike?" Elizabeth asked.

"I had my mom drop me off tonight." They walked out of the park.

"I have a flashlight," said Elizabeth.

"Great."

As they got farther from the ball fields, Justin seemed to relax. "Did you get in trouble last night?" he asked.

"Mom was reading when I got home, and I don't think she even noticed that I was late," said Elizabeth. "Did you find out anything else from your computer newspaper?"

"The what?" Justin looked like he didn't have any idea what she was talking about.

"You know. That thing you were talking about last night, the Bat A. Thousand thing."

"The computer bulletin board! Somebody said there's going to be a raffle of a Pete White card at the appearance on Saturday. Can you imagine him turning up after all these years?"

"That's what Mr. Becker said too," said Elizabeth. She had to find out about her baseball card before someone won it in a drawing!

The two of them slowed as they approached the baseball card shop.

"We'll walk by and make sure there aren't any lights on, then we'll go around back, okay?" Elizabeth said.

"He said he was going home, right?"

"But someone else could be in there. Jim, for instance."

From the front, the card shop was completely dark except for a red exit sign shining above the doorway to the back of the shop.

They turned into the alley. The dumpster had been moved closer to the door of the shop, leaving the space between the two buildings clear. Elizabeth took the flashlight out of the back pack and flicked it on.

"Not yet!" Justin whispered. "Make sure there's nobody in the back of the store."

She turned the light off.

Elizabeth and Justin walked in the shadows, staying close to the walls of the buildings lining the alley. They stopped before they reached the card shop.

"I'll check the dumpster," said Justin, holding out his hand.

Elizabeth gave him the flashlight.

While he shined the light on the ground around the dumpster, Elizabeth approached one of the two windows facing the alley. At first, it appeared to be covered with dirt. She tried to rub a small spot clean and realized that the window had been painted over.

"Darn!"

Elizabeth turned around, and Justin was hanging half in and half out of the dumpster.

"It's completely empty. The garbage collectors must have come by today." He dropped to the ground.

Moving to the second window, Elizabeth pressed her face against the screen and peered into the back room. The room was lit with a soft red glow she suspected was another exit sign like they'd seen in the front of the shop. She moved away from the screen to make room for Justin to have a look, and the screen followed her, clattering to the ground.

Elizabeth jumped back, knocking into Justin who grabbed her and pulled her behind the dumpster.

"It was the screen," Elizabeth whispered, her mouth so dry her lips could scarcely form the words. Justin let go of her arms. She leaned against the dumpster, her heart continuing to beat so loudly she was sure Justin must hear it.

"The store must be empty if no one came out to see what that was," Justin said in a normal voice.

The two of them returned to the window. Without the screen covering it, Elizabeth noticed that the bottom window was slightly raised. She stuck her hand under the sash and pushed upward. As the window moved, Justin nodded, encouraging her to raise it higher.

"We can't!" Elizabeth said when she realized he intended that they go inside.

"We didn't find anything out here. And if you want proof …"

Elizabeth tried to think of another way, but

she came up blank. She pushed the window as far as it would go, then stepped in the basket Justin made with his hands and slipped inside.

The room was very dark. The red light cast an eerie glow over the boxes and pieces of furniture scattered around the room. Elizabeth moved away from the window and stood perfectly still waiting for Justin.

The window was narrow and Justin had to twist and turn to get himself through the opening. Once in, he pulled the flashlight out of his pocket and ran it over the room.

Suddenly, the door under the red light swung open.

10
PRISONERS IN A HOUSE OF CARDS

Mr. Becker squinted when the light hit his eyes, then moved his hand up to shade them. "How'd you get in here?" he demanded. His eyes darted around the room as Elizabeth tried to make herself as small as possible. His eyes stopped and focused right above her head—on the open window, she realized.

"We were looking for my Pete White card," Elizabeth burst out. "This isn't it." She pulled the fake card out of the front pocket of her backpack. "I know that you and Mr. Hamilton had something to do with switching it."

Mr. Becker laughed.

Elizabeth had expected him to run for the door or get angry. She hadn't expected laughter.

"And what leads you to believe that I am the villain?" Mr. Becker asked.

"I found this in your dumpster." Elizabeth tossed the card she'd found the night before on the floor in front of Mr. Becker. "Shine the light on the floor," Elizabeth said to Justin.

Elizabeth started to edge slowly toward the door, her eyes fixed on Mr. Becker. She hadn't gone far when she stepped on something squishy just as Justin cried out, "My foot!"

Before she knew what was happening, Mr. Becker grabbed Elizabeth's wrist. "Wouldn't want you to fall," he said.

"Bobby, what's going on out here?" An old man bent over a cane hobbled out of the small room that opened under the red light.

When the man looked up and Elizabeth saw who it was, she quit struggling to get away.

"You're Pete White!" Justin said in an awe-struck voice.

Pete White didn't answer. He looked at Mr. Becker.

"Trying to get an advance peek?" said Mr. Becker. He patted Pete White on the shoulder. "This *is* Pete White."

Justin shined the flashlight over the old man. Elizabeth kept her eyes on the old man's eyes. They were brown, not blue. Who was trying to fool whom in this mess? Had Mr. Hamilton's friend been wrong, been lying?

"These your kids, Bobby?" the old man asked. "Right handsome family you have." He grinned at Elizabeth and Justin.

"Mr. White, I am so pleased to meet you," Justin said, holding his hand out to the man.

Again, Pete White looked at Mr. Becker. Elizabeth could see his face clearly now that her eyes had adjusted to the dim light. She thought he looked confused.

"Bobby, why do they keep calling me Mr. White?" the man asked in a whiny voice.

Mr. Becker's grip tightened on Elizabeth's wrist, and she groaned.

"What am I going to do with you kids now?" Mr. Becker asked.

"We're sorry, Mr. Becker, for trying to get a sneak preview. Elizabeth thought she'd lost something at the card show, and we were wrong not to ask about it," said Justin. "You can call our parents, whatever. Just let go of Elizabeth."

Mr. Becker laughed. "John, go out in front and wait for me."

"Okay, Bobby." The old man moved slowly toward the front room. When he reached the curtain, he turned. "Pete White. I'm supposed to pretend I'm a baseball player tonight?"

"Old fool," Mr. Becker whispered.

Elizabeth looked at Justin and knew they were thinking the same thing.

"Pete White had blue eyes," she said as the old man moved behind the curtain.

"And how many people are going to remember that? Not everyone is the expert on Pete White that you are," Mr. Becker said. "I thought if I fixed your card you'd never know. Couldn't take a chance on you showing up on Saturday, waving that around. Besides, it should belong to someone who really appreciates it. Like me."

"I'm not the only one who knows about the eyes," said Elizabeth.

"Yeah?"

Elizabeth shut up. Please God, help us, she prayed silently. Don't let me say anything that makes him any madder.

Mr. Becker pulled her closer. Justin took a step toward him.

"I'm okay," Elizabeth said to Justin as Mr. Becker's fingers dug into her flesh.

Justin leapt forward, swinging at the bigger man. With one arm, Mr. Becker pushed him backward into a stack of boxes. "I wouldn't try that again if I were you," he warned, lifting Elizabeth's arm and twisting it slightly.

Elizabeth stifled a groan.

"You two have created a big problem for me, and I need a minute to figure out how to solve it. It's just as well it's come to this. I was thinking about getting out of this place anyway, and you've made me come to a decision. I'll just move my departure timetable forward a little.

"Maybe you've even done me a favor," he continued. "In a new town, I can use the same cards all over again while I'm building my little nest egg. That would be most satisfactory. But after ... after ..."

Roughly, Mr. Becker pulled Elizabeth over to the open door. "Ladies first," he said before pushing her inside.

Elizabeth landed against the sharp edge of a table. She rubbed her arm where Mr. Becker had held her. Justin walked in behind her, pulling away when Mr. Becker touched his shoulder.

"I'll be back to take care of the two of you later. I'd better get Uncle Johnny home before we have any other visitors. But don't worry, I'll be back. I'm not going to let anyone, especially a couple of snotty kids, keep me from making this last big play. In fact, with all the excitement over the disappearance of two of the town's fairest children, who's going to notice whether Pete

White has blue eyes or brown?"

The door slammed, and Elizabeth heard the lock click.

"You should have let me buy the card," Mr. Becker said through the closed door.

"C'mon, Uncle Johnny. We'll go to McDonald's on the way home, and you can have some fries," Elizabeth heard him say to the old man.

She slumped against the table top. Her first impulse was to scream and scream until someone showed up to let them out of the small dark room. Instead, she closed her eyes and whispered, "Please, Jesus, help us get out of here."

"Where are you?" Justin whispered.

"Over here."

"What are you doing?"

"Praying," said Elizabeth.

"Pray for me too," Justin said.

Elizabeth started guiltily. She knew Jesus could save her from anything—that He'd even gone to the cross to save her. Get us both out of here, she continued praying. And Jesus, help me tell Justin about Your love.

When Elizabeth opened her eyes, she still couldn't see Justin, but she heard him breathing. Very carefully, she felt her way along the edge of the table. After awhile, she decided it was a countertop. When she reached the wall, Elizabeth moved her hand up and across, finally finding a light switch. She flipped it up.

Expecting the room to be flooded with light, Elizabeth was taken aback when a small light came on above a sink. The light cast a sickly orange glow over everything in sight.

"A darkroom!" said Justin. "Look at all the equipment!"

The room was small enough for Elizabeth to see almost everything in one glance. She wasn't interested in what the pieces of equipment were—she wanted to find a way out.

"It was Mr. Becker. I can't believe it," said Justin, picking up a stack of cards and shuffling through them. "Look at this. I bought this one for $12 and thought I was buying the real thing. Here's another one I bought from him. Oh, man. My collection is worthless. All these copies. They're fakes. They're all fakes!"

As Elizabeth listened to Justin, she tried to get rid of the feeling that she was overlooking something. The darkroom was built in the back corner of the building. Elizabeth lurched forward, tapping on the wall over the sink.

"What are you doing?" Justin asked.

"The second window, the one that was painted over. It should be somewhere in this room." Elizabeth continued to knock.

"There! Stop!" Justin said.

She knocked again and listened carefully. It did sound a little different. Elizabeth moved her fingers along the seams of the cheap wood paneling nailed above the countertop. She found a buckle in the wood and worked her fingers inside. The wood parted from the wall with a pop. Behind the paneling was the window.

"Good thing Mr. Becker left," said Justin. "He would have heard that for sure." Justin pulled another piece of paneling loose, and they backed away to see what they'd uncovered.

"He must have painted over it thinking that would keep the light out, and when it didn't, he covered it with wood," said Justin.

"Lucky for us Mr. Becker's a better con man and counterfeiter than he is a carpenter," said Elizabeth.

Justin pushed up on the window, but it didn't budge. Elizabeth joined him, but it was stuck tight.

"We'll have to break it," said Justin.

"Break it!" Elizabeth backed away. "If we do that, we'll get in trouble."

"Elizabeth," Justin said in a soft voice, "we are in trouble."

"You're right. Break it."

"You break it," said Justin.

"We have to do it quietly," said Elizabeth. Even though she'd heard him leave, she worried that Mr. Becker might have come back and was waiting for them in the alley.

"Give me your shirt," she said to Justin.

"What?"

"You have a T-shirt under it, don't you?"

"Yes, but ..."

"I want to do this sort of quietly," said Elizabeth.

Justin handed her the shirt. Elizabeth wrapped it around a metal tray and punched the glass. It shattered. Elizabeth and Justin jumped back.

"The shirt didn't make it much quieter," said Justin.

Quickly, Elizabeth used the tray to knock all the jagged pieces of glass out of the frame, then swept the shards onto the floor.

"I hope I'll fit through that opening," said Justin.

"Just come on," said Elizabeth as she easily climbed out.

She shifted her weight from one foot to the other, as Justin tried to fit through first one way then another. When he finally got all the way through, she grabbed his hand and started running toward the end of the alley.

"Where are we going?" Justin asked.

"To the police station. It's across the railroad tracks and down the next block."

Justin stopped, and Elizabeth almost fell backward.

"What are you waiting for? He may come back any minute!" she shouted at him.

"You think we're going to walk into the police station and tell them this story and they're going to believe us?" asked Justin.

"Why not?"

"We're kids," said Justin.

Elizabeth thought about what he'd said.

"Then we need to get the police to come to the shop some other way," she said slowly.

"How are we going to do that?" Justin's voice was getting higher and higher.

"Is there a pay phone anywhere near the baseball card shop?" Elizabeth asked.

"There's one at the train station," said Justin.

"You go to the phone and call 911. Tell them you see smoke coming out of the back of the card shop. Then hurry back, and I'll be inside the darkroom. I'll put the paneling back and every-thing. When the firemen come in and find me locked in that room, they'll have to believe us!"

"You go make the phone call, and I'll go back to the room," said Justin. "Who knows what Mr. Becker had planned for us?"

"You'll never get back inside. You had a hard enough time getting out. Just do it!" Eliza-beth turned and ran down the alley.

The window seemed to open into an eerie world. Elizabeth hesitated, trying to come up with something else that might work. She remembered her dad's baseball card and how he beamed each time he showed it to her. She couldn't let Mr. Becker take that away from her. Not to mention parading a Pete White who was-n't even Pete White in front of the whole world. She scrambled over the ledge, feeling a piece of glass stab into the palm of her hand.

Ignoring the pain, Elizabeth replaced the pieces of paneling and leaned them against the wall. She removed her shoe and pounded the remaining nails back into place as quickly as she could. When she finished that, Elizabeth turned off the light and sat down to wait for the police.

The darkness magnified the silence. And once she sat down, Elizabeth remembered the piece of glass in her hand. It stung and ached. She ran the fingers of her other hand over it and felt the edges sticking out.

Elizabeth heard a faint knocking on the window. She stood up.

"Are you okay?" Justin asked.

"Fine," said Elizabeth, wishing Justin was inside the room with her.

The wail of a siren reverberated off the close-set buildings as the emergency vehicles turned down the alley.

"Here! Here!" Elizabeth heard Justin's voice.

There was a pounding on the back door so strong that Elizabeth felt it as much as heard it.

"Fire department!" a man's voice shouted.

Running footsteps passed the darkroom from the front of the shop.

"What's going on? What's the meaning of this?"

Elizabeth was surprised to hear Mr. Becker's voice. When had he come back? She pounded on the dark room door. "Help! Help! Let me out of here! He's holding me prisoner!"

11
ELIZABETH SHOWS HER CARDS

When the door finally opened, Elizabeth stumbled out of the room, her eyes assaulted by the bright lights. When she could see, she noticed Mr. Becker arguing with a police officer. Several firemen were searching the building, and Mr. Hamilton stood in the doorway between the front and back rooms. When he saw Elizabeth, his mouth dropped open.

Mr. Hamilton crossed the room in two strides and grabbed Elizabeth by the arm. "What were you doing in there? Are you all right?"

Elizabeth pulled away. "He locked us up. We surprised him and Pete White and found proof that he's been counterfeiting baseball cards. He was trying to keep us quiet." The room was suddenly silent.

"Just one minute, little lady." The police officer turned toward Elizabeth.

"He, Mr. Becker, took a very valuable base-ball card out of my purse. He made a counterfeit copy of it but changed the eye color of the player and put it in place of the real one. He thought I wouldn't notice, but I did." She looked at Mr. Hamilton. "Well, I didn't notice exactly, but I knew something was wrong with it."

"So that's what he did! He doesn't have Pete White at all!" said Mr. Hamilton.

"And he might be in on it too," Elizabeth said pointing to Mr. Hamilton. "Ask him where he got the money for the baseball trip."

"Now wait a minute. I thought something funny was going on here too. Eric and I have been doing a little investigating of our own. I set up an appointment with Mr. Becker to try to get some information. However, we went to the police and told them what we suspected rather than trying to prove it on our own," said Mr. Hamilton.

"And as for the money, I sold some of the dark-room equipment from my home. Since I can use the high school's dark room, I don't need all that expensive stuff taking up space. I decided to sell it so the kids wouldn't miss out on a great opportunity and a fun trip."

Elizabeth looked, embarrassed, from Mr.

Hamilton to the police officer. She didn't know what to think now.

"You might consider doing as Mr. Hamilton did the next time you think there's a problem," the police officer said. "Never try to handle trouble on your own. Call us right away." The officer took Elizabeth's hand and started to lead her to a chair.

"Ow!" Elizabeth couldn't help crying out. He'd grabbed it right where the glass was stuck.

"Get a paramedic in here," the officer said to one of the firemen. "How did this happen?"

"We broke out a window in there," Elizabeth pointed to the darkroom.

"But you were still inside," Mr. Hamilton said, looking confused.

"We didn't know if anyone would believe our story," said Justin.

The paramedic examined Elizabeth's hand. "Better take her to the ER," she said. "This is going to need stitches."

"I'll call your mom and have her meet us there," said Mr. Hamilton.

Justin was talking to the police officer, explaining about the stacks of counterfeit cards in the darkroom, the card Elizabeth had found in the dumpster, and the old man who looked like Pete White.

Mr. Becker glared at Elizabeth, Justin, and Mr. Hamilton in turn. "He's my uncle, and he doesn't have a clue what's going on. I needed money to get him into a retirement home. He's senile and needs more care than I can give him."

Elizabeth felt sorry for the old man. She doubted that Mr. Becker planned to use much of the money he made off of "Pete White" to take care of his uncle. Or maybe she was wrong. Mr. Becker had to be awfully desperate to do what he was planning to do.

As soon as Mr. Hamilton hung up the phone, he had a hushed conversation with the police officer. The two of them approached Elizabeth.

"I'm releasing you for now," the officer said to her. "But I'll need you to come to the station to give us a statement. I'll also need your solemn promise never to do anything like this on your own again. It's our job to catch criminals. Your job is to ...," the officer stopped and looked thoughtful for a minute, "to be a kid."

12

Honestly, It's Just a Date

"Five stitches, that's all." Elizabeth held out her bandaged hand for Justin to see.

"That's all! That's quite enough, I'll have you know," Aunt Nan said. "I thank God that you're safe and sound."

"That's five too many," added Mom.

"I had stitches once," said Mike.

"So what did they do with Mr. Becker?" Elizabeth asked.

"They arrested him. There was plenty of evidence in that room where he locked us up," said Justin. "And they took his uncle to the nursing home down the street for now. It was lucky for us that Mr. Hamilton had made that appointment to meet Mr. Becker at the shop."

Mom put her arm around Elizabeth's shoulders. "Please, the thought of the two of you ..."

Elizabeth felt her Mom shudder.

A black Volvo pulled up to the curb, and Mr. Hamilton honked the horn. "Can somebody come down here and help me carry this ice cream?"

"Ice cream! Oh, boy!" Mike was off the porch and at the car in a flash.

Thoughts of Mr. Hamilton with his arm around her mother flooded Elizabeth's mind. That's what had happened at the hospital the night before. When they'd finished stitching her hand and rolled her out to the waiting room, they'd been waiting for her—Mr. Hamilton and Mom, sitting so close together there was no place for her. Every time she thought about it, it was like a hole opened up in the middle of her chest and cold air and ice rushed to fill it.

"I was at the station this morning. You'll eventually get the Pete White card back, after the case against Mr. Becker is closed. That's good news, isn't it, Elizabeth?" Mr. Hamilton said.

Elizabeth shrugged.

"Can't you tell us what your friend Mr. Sommers found out about the real Pete White?" Justin asked Mr. Hamilton.

"I asked him, and he did say I could tell you—*if* Elizabeth will let him use the Pete White baseball card in his book."

"Of course he can," Mom said before Elizabeth could answer.

"It's what I'd always suspected," said Mr. Hamilton. "White lived on a farm in Nebraska during the off-season, his dad's farm, and he helped out whenever he could. Unfortunately, he got into an argument with a combine and he lost—his arm, his pitching arm."

Elizabeth shuddered. "But he didn't die?"

"Not then. He lived in seclusion, not telling anyone for many years. He couldn't bear the thought of facing his teammates and fans."

"Didn't anybody look for him when he disappeared?" asked Justin.

"His family respected his wishes and denied any knowledge of his whereabouts," explained Mr. Hamilton. "However, he died two years ago, and when Eric retraced the investigation, he found someone willing to talk."

"Amazing," said Aunt Nan.

Elizabeth found the story depressing. The interest in the fake Pete White made her feel sure that people would have accepted the real man, with or without his arm.

"When will the book be published?" Justin asked.

"Next spring," said Mr. Hamilton.

"I can't wait," said Justin. "But right now I have papers to deliver. See you tomorrow, Elizabeth?"

She nodded and managed to smile at him.

"That boy forgot to deliver our paper!" Aunt Nan said as Justin rode away.

Mom brought a handful of spoons out and stuck them into the sundaes Mr. Hamilton had brought them.

Mr. Hamilton sat down on the opposite end of the porch swing from Elizabeth. After she passed out the spoons, Mom sat down between the two of them, squishing Elizabeth into the corner.

Mike was talking to Mr. Hamilton about the baseball team, and Mom and Aunt Nan were discussing whether they needed to water the garden or not.

The cats, Tiger and Delores, slowly approached the porch and sniffed the bag the ice cream came in.

"Here, kitty," Elizabeth called to them. "Kitty, kitty."

Tiger glanced her way, then jumped onto Mr. Hamilton's lap. Not to be outdone, Delores joined him.

"They always know the one who doesn't want them around," Aunt Nan said. "Push them off."

"Go on. Get away," Mom said to the cats.

"Leave 'em alone," said Mr. Hamilton. "They aren't so bad."

"This from the man who called them over-grown rodents," Elizabeth mumbled.

"What did you say?" Mom asked. "Did you see this? Can you believe Delores is actually sitting on his lap?" Delores never sat on anyone's lap except Elizabeth's. She slept on Elizabeth's bed and lived in Elizabeth's room. She was Elizabeth's cat through and through—until now.

Elizabeth could hear the traitor purring from her end of the swing.

"Are you feeling all right, honey?" Mom asked.

"My hand is hurting, and I feel kind of, I don't know, hot and achy all over," Elizabeth said, exaggerating a bit.

"Go inside and take some Tylenol and maybe rest a little. Don and I are going to a movie and then to dinner. Aunt Nan will be here if you need anything," said Mom.

Elizabeth stood up. Her mother was going to leave her home alone when she was feeling bad. Tears stung Elizabeth's eyes.

As she went upstairs, Elizabeth could still hear laughter on the front porch. She took Tylenol, then laid down on her bed, wishing that Delores was with her now. Even the cat had chosen Mr. Hamilton.

"Lizzybeth?"

Elizabeth kept her eyes closed.

Mom came over and sat on the side of the bed. "Do you want me to stay home with you? We can go to the movies and dinner another night."

"You've never gone out on a date before," Elizabeth said, tears running out of the corners of her eyes into her hair.

Mom gently wiped them away. "I'm almost as surprised as you are, sweetie. But Don is a nice man, and he makes me laugh. Mike likes him and Aunt Nan. I think if you'd give him a chance, you might too."

"But what about Daddy?"

"This doesn't have anything to do with Daddy," Mom said gently. "I'll always love Daddy and you. Honestly, it's just a date."

Elizabeth's smile quivered. "Go on. Aunt Nan will take good care of me."

Mom kissed Elizabeth's forehead. "I know she will. You rest now."

As Mom stood up, Delores jumped onto the foot of the bed.

Elizabeth patted the spot beside her, and the cat immediately settled in.